Mr. Putter & Tabby Stir the Soup

MACARONI
ELBOW
MACARONI

CYNTHIA RYLANT

Mr. Putter & Tabby Stir the Soup

Illustrated by
ARTHUR HOWARD

sandpiper
Houghton Mifflin Harcourt
Boston New York

For Michael, Debra, Rebecca, Sophia, and Nina
—A. H.

www.hmhbooks.com

First Harcourt paperback edition 2004

Library of Congress Cataloging-in-Publication Data
Rylant, Cynthia.
Mr. Putter & Tabby stir the soup/Cynthia Rylant;
illustrated by Arthur Howard.
p. cm.
Summary: Mr. Putter and Tabby go to their neighbor's house
to make soup, but Zeke the dog makes it very difficult for them.
[1. Soups—Fiction. 2. Cats—Fiction. 3. Dogs—Fiction.
4. Neighbors—Fiction.] I. Title: Mr. Putter and Tabby stir the soup.
II. Howard, Arthur, ill. III. Title.
PZ7.R982Mud 2003
[E]—dc21 2002011387
ISBN: 978-0-15-202637-0 hardcover
ISBN: 978-0-15-205058-0 paperback

Manufactured in China
LEO 20 19 18 17 16 15 14 13 12 11
4500317635

1

Soup Day

Mr. Putter and his fine cat, Tabby,
lived in an old house
with an old porch
and an old swing
and lots of old things inside.
Mr. Putter and Tabby
didn't mind old things.
They were old, too,
so they felt right at home.

One of the oldest things in
Mr. Putter's house
was the stove.
Mr. Putter was very attached
to his stove.
He called her Bessie.

Every day Bessie cooked up
oatmeal and tea for
Mr. Putter and Tabby.

Some days she
cooked up muffins.

And on really special days,
she cooked up soup.
Mr. Putter and Tabby *loved* soup.

But it was a lot of trouble.
Mr. Putter never had all the
right ingredients at the right time.
"No onions," he would say to Tabby.
"No soup."
Or, "No beans," he would say.
"No soup."

And sometimes:
"No macaroni. No soup."
Tabby was really sorry
about the macaroni.
It was her favorite part.

But one day when Mr. Putter
and Tabby wanted soup,
Mr. Putter found he had *everything*.

"Look, Tabby," said Mr. Putter.
"Even macaroni!"
Tabby purred and purred.
Today would be a soup day.

2

Maybe Not

Mr. Putter put everything on the counter and started chopping.
He chopped up celery.
He chopped up carrots.
He chopped up potatoes.
He chopped up onions and cried and cried.

Tabby worried and rubbed
against his legs.
"Don't worry, Tabby,"
said Mr. Putter.
"It's just the onions."
He smiled and gave her a pat.
Tabby felt much better.

Mr. Putter dumped all of the
chopped things into a big
pot of water.

He turned on the stove
to let them cook.
But nothing happened.
Bessie didn't warm up.
She didn't warm up even a little.
She just sat there, cold and quiet.
"Oh no," said Mr. Putter. "Bessie's
on the blink. Now what do we do?"

Mr. Putter looked at Tabby.
Tabby looked at Mr. Putter.
They both looked at Mrs. Teaberry's
house through the window.
"Hmmm," said Mr. Putter.

3

Neighbors

Mrs. Teaberry was Mr. Putter's friend.
Her good dog, Zeke, was Tabby's friend.
They all liked being neighbors.
And Mrs. Teaberry *loved* to cook.

"Maybe Mrs. Teaberry will help us
make soup," said Mr. Putter.
He phoned her up.

"Mrs. Teaberry," said Mr. Putter,
"Bessie's on the blink, and I'm
trying to make soup."
"Oh dear," said Mrs. Teaberry.
"May Tabby and I make soup at your house?"
asked Mr. Putter.

"Well," said Mrs. Teaberry, "I'm just on my way out to shuck oysters with the girls."

(Mrs. Teaberry enjoyed odd things.)

"Can you make your soup with Zeke in the house?" she asked.

"Of course," said Mr. Putter.

"He'll be good," said Mrs. Teaberry.

"Of course," said Mr. Putter.

"He'll be nice," said Mrs. Teaberry.

"Of course," said Mr. Putter.

"And he promises not to be a bother,"
said Mrs. Teaberry.

"Oh, Zeke's not a bother," said Mr. Putter.
"We'll be right over!"

4

The Bother

Mr. Putter and Tabby carried
all of their soup things over
to Mrs. Teaberry's house.
Zeke met them at the door.
He had his leash.
"No walk, Zeke," said Mr. Putter.

He and Tabby went into the kitchen.
Zeke came in with his ball.
"No ball, Zeke," said Mr. Putter.

Mr. Putter started chopping tomatoes.
Zeke came in with his stick.
"No stick, Zeke," said Mr. Putter.

Mr. Putter started chopping turnips.
Zeke came in with a potted plant.
"Jiminy!" said Mr. Putter.
Mr. Putter and Tabby chased Zeke
all over Mrs. Teaberry's house.

Finally Zeke gave up the plant.
Mr. Putter put it in the bathtub
where Zeke couldn't reach it.
"No plant, Zeke," said Mr. Putter.

He and Tabby went back to the kitchen.
Mr. Putter started chopping parsley.
Zeke came in with a radio.
"Jiminy!" said Mr. Putter.

Mr. Putter and Tabby chased Zeke
all over Mrs. Teaberry's house.

Finally Zeke gave up the radio.
Mr. Putter and Tabby went back
to the kitchen.

Zeke came in with a lamp.

"Jiminy!" said Mr. Putter.

It was a very interesting morning.

5

Soup

When Mrs. Teaberry finally got home,
Mr. Putter was asleep,
Tabby was asleep, and
Zeke was eating a carrot.
"Oh dear," said Mrs. Teaberry.
Her house looked a little different.
It was *missing* things.

HOW TO TRAIN YOOR PET!

She looked through all of the rooms.

Then she looked in the bathtub.

"Oh dear," she said.

Mrs. Teaberry looked at Zeke.

"Were you a bother?" she asked.

Zeke wagged.

Mrs. Teaberry went into the kitchen.
Poor Mr. Putter.
His soup was still not cooked,
and there was a lamp in
the kitchen sink.

Mrs. Teaberry got to work.
She made raisin bread and
chocolate fudge and
melted cheese toasties.
And she stirred Mr. Putter's soup
all afternoon.

When Mr. Putter woke up,
they had the most wonderful
meal—and the best soup Mr. Putter
and Tabby had ever tasted!
"I'm sorry Zeke was a bother,"
said Mrs. Teaberry.

"Oh," said Mr. Putter,

"Zeke is *never* a bother..."

"But have you seen my hat?"

The illustrations in this book were done in pencil, watercolor,
and gouache on 250-gram cotton rag paper.
The display type was set in Minya Nouvelle, Agenda, and Artcraft.
The text type was set in Berkeley Old Style Book.
Color separations by Colourscan Co. Pte. Ltd., Singapore
Printed by LEO, China
Production supervision by Sandra Grebenar and Pascha Gerlinger
Series cover design by Kristine Brogno and Michele Wetherbee
Cover design by Brad Barrett
Designed by Arthur Howard and Judythe Sieck